ROWAN

by Robin McKinley

pictures by Donna Ruff

Greenwillow Books New York

A combination of airbrush, pastels, and
colored pencils was used for the full-color art.
The text type is Breughel No. 55.

Printed in Singapore by Tien Wah Press
First Edition
1 2 3 4 5 6 7 8 9 10

Library of Congress Cataloging-in-Publication Data
McKinley, Robin.
Rowan / by Robin McKinley;
pictures by Donna Ruff.
p.   cm.
Summary: A child and a new puppy work through
the difficult initial adjustments and soon
belong to each other.
ISBN 0-688-10682-X (trade).
ISBN 0-688-10683-8 (lib.)
[1. Dogs—Fiction.   I. Ruff, Donna, ill.
II. Title. PZ7.M1988Ro 1992
[E]—dc20 91-31809 CIP AC

JP

FOR CINDY,
WHO DID IT FIRST

—R. McK.

FOR ERIC, FOR LORIN,
AND FOR WILLY

—D. R.

I didn't know I wanted a dog. And then, one day, I did know. I did want a dog.

I read dog books. I talked to dog people. I looked at the ads under PETS in the newspaper. But I didn't see what I wanted.

It would have been easier if I had known what I wanted.

German shepherds were strong and intelligent. But maybe too strong.

Irish wolfhounds were big and gentle. But maybe too big.

Golden retrievers were hairy and friendly. But maybe too hairy.

I was at the dentist's one day, because I had a toothache. I was in a bad mood because of the toothache. I read the pets column in the dentist's newspaper while I was waiting.

WHIPPET PUPS, it said.

A whippet, I thought. A whippet is intelligent and friendly and gentle. It's not too big and it's not too hairy and it's not too strong.

I was so busy thinking about my puppy, I almost didn't mind having my tooth fixed.

I went to see the puppies the next day.

I knew mine at once. She sprang up when I first bent over her, and kissed me on the nose. She ran like a fawn, and chewed her brothers' ears and my fingers.

She was white with brindle patches: both ears, one eye, one shoulder, a few ribs, the base of her tail. And one silly black spot that looked like it fell off a Dalmatian on the back of her neck.

She wagged her tail so hard and fast, I looked for a wind-up key in her back that I could turn when she ran down, like a plastic dog in a toy store.

But she only fell on my feet, and as I rubbed her tummy, her tail went as fast as ever.

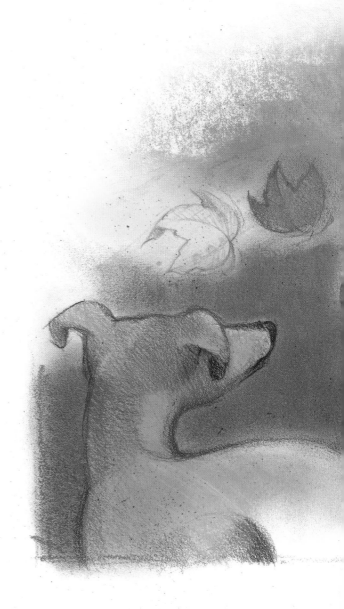

I named her Rowan. And I brought
her home with me.

She threw up—twice—on the long drive. She was very miserable. I was glad we had extra newspapers with us.

We stopped once and got out of the car. I thought fresh air might make her feel better. It had started to rain.

I stood in the long grass by the side of the road. Rowan crept between my legs to get out of the rain, and waited to be carried back to the nice, dry car.

She was very quiet when I brought her into my house. She didn't know anything about houses, and carpets, and furniture, and telephones. She walked through the house, staying very close to me.

She looked up at me, often and sadly. I had taken her away from everything she knew, but I was all she had left. I was sad because she was sad. She didn't even wag her tail.

She drank some water, but she wouldn't eat any dinner.

I brought her bed into my bedroom when it was time to go to sleep. Every few minutes she stood up and whirled herself into a new little curl. Every time she stood up and spun around, I woke up.

In the morning I was still tired, and unhappy because my puppy was unhappy. But when I sat up and put my feet on the floor, she sat up, too, and looked at me.

"Hello, Rowan," I said.

And she flattened her little ears and wagged the tip—just the tip—of her long tail at me.

But when I bent over her, she lifted her little face
and gave me wet puppy kisses on my big face.

So I knew she was mine, after all.

And I was hers.